IIIIIIIIIIIIIIIIIIIIIIIIIIIIIIIII
I0551484

Fragments of

a

Fading

Dream

Latasha Monique

Lorraine Day

Latasha Monique Lorraine Day

Copyright © 2012 Latasha Monique Lorraine Day

All rights reserved.

Text, Artwork & Cover Design by Latasha Day

ISBN: 0615734170
ISBN-13: 978-0615734170

DEDICATION

This book is dedicated to those whom I have loved, those whom I have lost, and those who live in my dreams

PREFACE

I lost myself in the fireworks that year. It was the 4th of July and I was 14 years old. I believed I died that night, and when I woke up, I was in a parallel universe. After about a week I was somewhat able to convince myself otherwise; but sometimes I still wonder how we know that our reality is real. How can we be sure that we are not just characters in someone else's dream; that there isn't another version of us out there somewhere, in a parallel world; an alternate reality. Every day we wake up and convince ourselves that this world is real; that it is somehow different from our dreams.
Because we have to, in order to live.

Lxa is a character who represents a version or an aspect of me; and although we may share some similarities, she is not me. The pieces included here tell her story but since it is not necessarily linear; it can be read in any order. There are a few consistent themes such as love, life, dreams, illusions, reality, memories and the distinctions between them.
This is her attempt to understand the world around her .

I hope that you enjoy this glimpse into the world of Lxa.

CONTENTS

Latasha Monique Lorraine Day

Lxa

My name, you ask

all I know is what they call me

I had a different one once

when I belonged to their world

but those days are distant memories

slowly fading into the fog

These days

it's hard to tell

the difference

between my reality

and theirs

I live most of my life
inside my head
trying to see the difference
between what is real and what
is not
what is simply my own creation
and what is outside of me
and whether or not
it matters

My walls are chalkboards
full of thoughts
trapped in my prison
words are my only friends
in my world of dreams
and memories
I write to help me understand
so hard to tell the difference,
locked in an illusion,
imprisoned in my own mind

I see the world underneath you
you know the difference
once I see, I can't see you at all
your words are all I know
I remember you
I see pictures of you
on my eyelids
are you in the dark?
Your words come back to haunt me
did it have to be this way?
You're not here anymore
you said it would be different

it was

your picture is cloudy

on my eyelids

now I see you as you were
before
if we could have said goodbye.

My eyelids can't see you anymore
but this isn't just memory
this is goodbye

maybe I'll wake up

I open my eyes

to emptiness

searching for pieces of me

lost long ago

and close them

to return

to the only place

that makes sense

Trapped in this prison
of my own making
searching for
my ultimate
escape
because no one
will ever
find me
hidden
in the dark recesses
of your heart

I live in between the lines

hidden in the shadows

of what you thought was there

you see straight thru me

cuz I don't fit

what you want me to be

I fall to pieces

just molecules

fading

before

your

eyes

As I look in the mirror
and try to really see
who is that person
looking back at me?
fading in and out
of reality
never knowing
which path to take
searching for freedom
in between the lines
I look at her
trapped in her prison
and wonder
if she will ever break free

Had a flashback
to a different time
a different life
and I wonder
where is she
that girl
I used to be
that girl
who had the whole world
ahead of her
who knew how to enjoy life
who always felt so alone
who often wondered
"what's the point of it all"
and who has finally
become
me

Sometimes I wish I didn't love you
because then
being away from you
wouldn't hurt so much

the connection that I feel to you
is so strong
please don't let it fade
with distance
we can't let it break
shatter like broken glass
I want you in my life
my future
I want for you
to be a part of
me

Pieces of me

folded up

on scraps of paper

hidden words

fading

trying

to put the pieces

back together

Dreams rise

from the ashes

of desire

and fuel the burning flame

and hold within

the memory

that we will rise

again

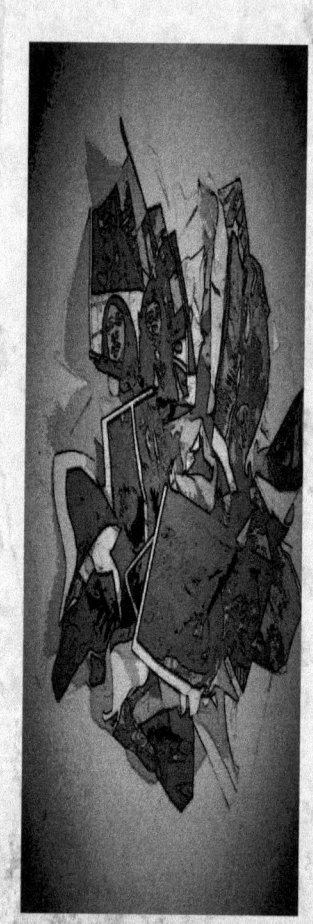

I am just a shade
of who I used to be
where is she?

Where do our dreams go?

Do they vanish if we let the world

prove us wrong

Nothing's ever gonna change

unless we escape this prison

some may call it society

but all it does is lock you in

buying into it only feeds the flame

What is a cloud?
If you pass through one,
does it change shape?
Or does it revert back
to its original form?
Does it have mass?
Or take up any space
is it wet? Or moist?
Why do they live
in the sky?

Dreamscape I

I find myself

floating

from one to the next

trying to find

an escape

trying to wake up

yet only opening

dream eyes

to different dreamscapes

unable to move the real ones

to return

to reality

Dreamscape II

My eyes are open now

I hear them talking

outside my door

I should be alone

hear glass breaking

– the mirrors on the wall

I find myself drinking

something thru a straw

and now their words are clear

I know they want to kill me

it's only a matter of time

until my real eyes open

and I realize

it must have been a dream

Dreamscape III

It is dark

I open my eyes

to see 3 sets of eyes

looking at me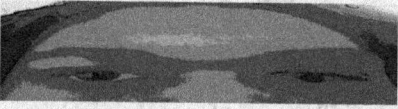

I chase them out

exhausted and scared

must have come in thru the window

and I awake

again

to find

they were never there

Dull pain consuming me

words will not come

to give me release

my monthly sentence

the baby that could have been

I think of her eyes

his smile

maybe one day

I will meet them

and they will forgive me

my sentence already served

Imprisoned

My heart is a prison

for you

I've trapped you there

holding you hostage

with every beat

I hold you there

because I know

if you escape

I will

die

you are

the only part

that keeps

me

alive

Emotions wash over me like waves

when they consume me

it feels like it will never end

but once they pass

& the sea is calm

it's as if

all that turmoil

never existed

you see I don't hold on

to pain

to anger

that sort of thing

and you are left wondering

what just happened!?

But by then, I've already moved on

lost in a sea

of calm serenity

Maybe consciousness

is what fills the empty space

the unifying field

and consciousness creates

not only how we see the world

but maybe the world itself

because the world is not outside of us

it is us

and changes as we change

If we can create change

within ourselves

then maybe it is possible

to change

the world

Lxa is what you can call me
but it is only a representation
just a reminder
that you can know my name
but still not see me
the L & the A represent the first & last
letters of my name
the X is the mystery that is in between
so now that you know my secret
have you learned anything?
If you knew from the beginning
would you have viewed me differently
would you have judged me
insubstantially
would that have shaped
your view of me
or would you be objective
in your pre-judgements
of who you perceive me to be
although, I think, that is impossible
being subjective is all that we can be,
all I ask
is for the chance
to show you who I am

I want you

    to kiss me

I want you

    to know me

I want you

    to be the 1

I share my heart with

Your love is so elusive
I can feel it
slipping through the palms of
my hands
I see us in the future
you see that I have been hurt
that I may not give my heart
so easily
to you
and you must prove
to me
that I am really
all
that you
want

Love:

Is not what we should be afraid of

is something we do

unconditionally

is what makes us human

what makes anything possible

& dreams come true

Is the basis of life

because without it

we withdraw

we wither

we die

Is a gift that we share

requiring nothing in return

fills our empty spaces

Is everything

and nothing

at once

I open my eyes this time

but not to see
all I feel
is you kissing me
your tongue on my skin
breasts, nipples
turning me on
stomach, thighs
then I feel your tongue

slip inside of me
licking me to ecstasy

I can still feel you
inside of me

Phoenix – Angel

She rose

from the ashes at her feet

watched them fall from her body

as she shed one tear

which turned to dust

and spread her wings

to let the wind

carry her

into the land

of her dreams

Do you believe

in a land of your dreams

where nothing

is as it seems

and none of our rules apply

Do you believe

that this place exists

and is very real

if only in our minds

what if

the world that we know

is only as real

in the larger sense

as this dream world

both equally

imaginary

Waking Dream

Imagine

waking to a nightmare

unable to see

your worst fears

so close to reality

what I knew in my heart

you refused to see

leaving me no other choice

but to break through

the walls

your unyielding rules

to reveal

what came as no surprise

to me

just the realization

that all my fears

had become reality

I cry tears of silk

sliding down my spider veins

looking in the mirror

at myself

sticky

stuck

caught in a web

of illusion

of my own creation

There is an airplane somewhere
with happiness written on its side
maybe if I find it
it can take me there

where there are angels,
and people made of clay
and voices that float around endlessly
everything is only as you want it to be
maybe I'll take you there someday
to this place inside my head

There is a place that I visit sometimes
possibly in my dreams
where strange things happen all the time
the rules of this world do not apply
nothing is as it seems
I may have seen you there before
maybe you'll remember

I am invisible, in the dark
they tell me you are there
but you can't see me
and I can't see you

why are we so blind?

Maybe in my land of dreams,
I'll see you once again

Happiness

is not something

you can give

or take

It is a force

in and of itself

it exists

inside of us

we just have to find it

within ourselves

Black ice

falling

like crystals from the sky

surrounding me

like pearls of desire

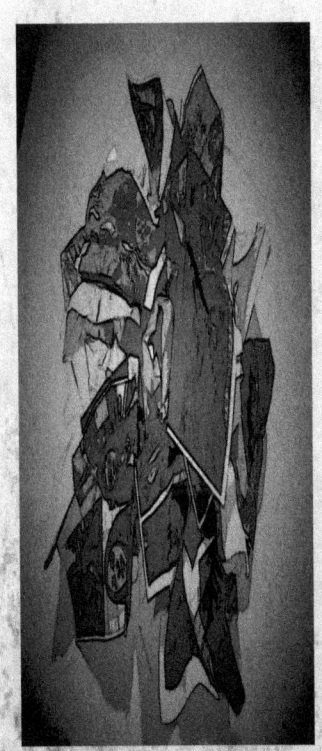

silver stains

floating

high above the skies

loving you

with tears in my eyes

That Weapon Called Love

Some like to hold it against you

use it like a threat

"you love me, don't you"

said with satisfaction

a sense of power

as if now they control you

and you just have to admit it

Love is something beautiful

why do some have to ruin it

how can someone

turn such a beautiful thing

into something

so

ugly

Missing

I wonder where you are
are you watching over me
can you see when I'm in pain
can you hear my cries for help
are you the 1 inside my head
telling me I'll be ok
or are you in the dark
wiping my tears away
standing by my side
through the times
when I need you most
are you there
when I close my eyes
& tell you what is in my heart
Do you know
how much I miss you
every day& every night
I wish that I could close my eyes
& bring you back to life

Am I the 1 who will always see
thru to the other side
holding u close
thru the flames
wishing u were the 1
to save me
this time around
hoping for the best
but knowing
in my heart
in my soul
that u & I
are always
the ones who
only find the truth
in the spaces
in between
the lines of our own story

I'm trusting you

with my heart, my soul

I'm hoping you will see

the real me

underneath

this masquerade

I am a work in progress

please don't judge

too harshly

what you cannot see

I want to believe

that you knew

from the start

that there is

something

between us

that I can't explain

but it's hard to see

what's in your heart

from this far

away

I can only trust

in your words

and hope

that truth

lies somewhere

in

between

Silent Kisses

The darkness turns towards me

& I face it

silently

waiting

for your image to appear

I walk towards you

& slowly reach out my hand

you pull me

softly

slowly

into you

and through your kisses

I am able to see

the light

Do you see me

in the dim light

are you in the same

plane as me

the same dimension

or string

of theories that make

up the reasons to be

holding U & I hostage

in the shadows

of the world to be

Close your eyes

& think of me

tell me what u see

am I strong

am I weak

am I what u seek?

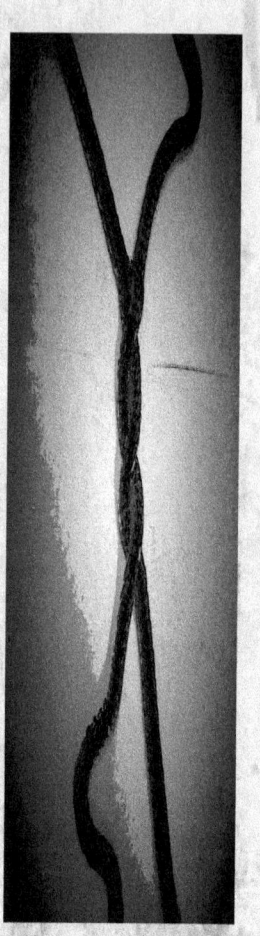

As the days go by
and years pass
I need to know
that we will be
ok
that we will survive
can u help me
to believe?

A thread
        then a string
then yarn
        and rope
to a solid chain
        linked together
never to be broken

You are my heart

my soul, my air

I breathe

you completely

feel you

inside me

your body

your soul

your spirit

the love you give me

I carry a part of you

in me

I need you

to help me remember

who I am

Now is a time for change
to put fear aside
and stand tall
to claim
what has always been yours

Do you find it strange
that I believe in love
that I know that happiness
is not only possible
but essential
to my survival
And I will survive
Did you know
that I can feel you
deep inside my bones
your smile gives me peace
a peace I feel whenever
you're on my mind
even though I can't see you
I know you're there
and I believe
in love

So nice holding you
breathing you
wishing this
would never end
not knowing where you end

and I

begin

Like an orgasm of calm
waves of pleasure
wash over me
I choose to ride
the waves
wherever
they may lead

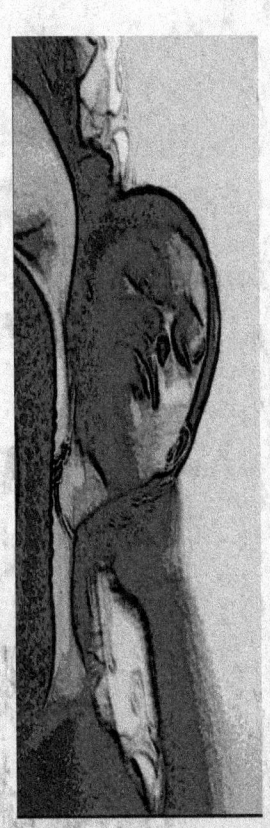

Love isn't something you find

it's something you do

it's not about ownership

or possession

or jealousy

or hate

or even passion

for that matter

it just is

and will

transcend

Imagine a river
of love
those who drink from it
are forever changed
the water in their bodies
slowly changes
causing changes
in their thoughts
their feelings
their DNA
changing their spirit
to one of love
& compassion
& understanding
& they will act
out of love
instead of
indifference
or
hate

It's always been hard for me

because I don't ask for help easily

and I don't give easy access

to myself

I guess it's easier to assume

that I'm okay

if only someone would ask

choose to look deeper,

behind my mask

they might see

I'm not always quite

what I seem

I never took the time

to get to know myself

until I was forced

to look myself

in the eye

and say that this

is who I am

flaws & all

nobody is perfect, but I do my best

to be the best person

that I can be

under any circumstances

and I will always

be

me

Many roads emerge

in the distance

all are paths

that I could take

destination: unknown

how can I create my own?

I remember

the taste of your kiss

the softness of your lips

your tongue

invading my mouth

sends sparks thru me

I can feel your hands

at my waist

undressing me

I can feel

the urgency

not knowing when

we'll meet again

I feel the passion

that we share

our bodies entwined

our spirit

as one

You now know that it is time

to finally

tear down the walls

that hold you back

but don't look back

don't turn around

like Orpheus & Eurydice

you have to believe in something

Cuz if you don't

you will lose everything

Not quite sure how it happened
            or what kind of voodoo
            that you do
                but you've somehow
            managed to
        get inside of me
            and yet
                still remain
            so distant,
                it seems.
        Why is it so surprising
    to you
            that I could want you,
miss you
                    even
    love you
            the way that I do
        I listen to your words as they become
                empty promises
                and I try
            to read between your lines
            and maybe I've been blind
but as they say
actions speak
much louder than words
so I don't wanna hear
            emptiness
            don't wanna wonder
                whether you're just tellin me
what you think
                I wanna hear

Masquerade

Close your eyes and watch
the darkness fade away
now that clouds no longer hide
their true faces
we're on the outside, looking in
unaware of the part we play
in the masquerade
look in the mirror, at your face
it's only a mask you wear
as time goes by
our masks begin to fade
and we begin to glimpse
the truth
our eyes are mirrors of the world
and as our masks are removed
one by one
our darkness turns to light

Spirit journey, soul guide

tell me what u have to hide

show me the way to truly be

all that I can

& will ever see

that the roads of life

are built for me

Maybe
I am learning to live
life in the present
and not the past
or the future
because today
is all we have
I can only change
how I feel today
and believe
in the prospects
for tomorrow

Maybe
I am learning to accept
life
as it is
without bitterness
and realize what's important
to me
and that the only limitations
are the ones that exist
in my own
mind

Birthday

Today
is my New Year's
Day
a time for beginnings
resolutions
a time for me
a time for
re-memory

I fantasize
about life
about love
about holding you close
about kissing your lips
tasting you
feeling your soul
inside of me
feeling your heart beat
in tune with mine
in my fantasy
you are the 1
who makes me cum

to my senses
to feel you
touch you
taste you
smell you
hear your soul
speak to mine
my fantasy
is for this
dream
to never
end

Before

I miss those days

who we were back then

with all the time in the world

all of our philosophical discussions

the secrets & lies

& unspoken truths

the days where

time was relative

our lives had yet to begin

how the ties unraveled

& shredded

the end of an era

and distance became real

Big Bang

If the universe is alive

is it an everlasting cycle?

what if the Big Bang

is not the beginning

just one of many

in the cycle

of life

Been waitin all night
for you
And you're still
not here

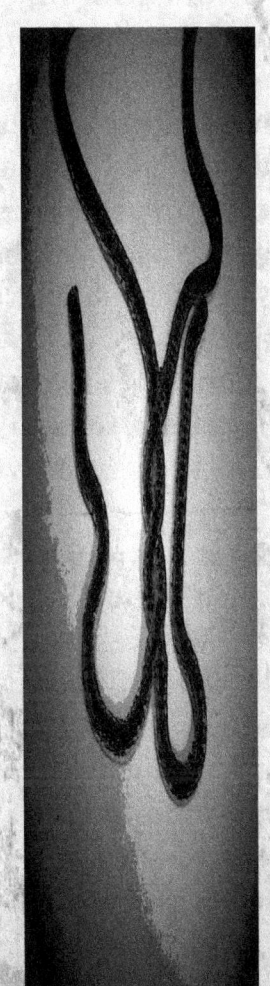

There are many soul mates
many we can love
all about timing
and making that decision
not love so much, although it helps
it's creating something
molding 2 lives into 1
we're so used to instability
expecting everything to be easy
when that's never been the case
giving up 2 easily
when times are rough
forgetting those 5 simple words
for better or for worse

but is a promise worth keeping
if you're not happy
almost like a contract
but is it still valid
if the initial terms weren't clear
maybe we need to know
the importance of communication
over assumption
never assume
that others feel
the same as you

Vow

I vow:

to be in charge of my own happiness

to make the decisions that are best for me

to speak my mind

to stand my ground

to be true to myself

to love myself, however imperfect

to forgive myself, for any wrongs

to remember that I am a work in progress

to realize, that I deserve the best

and that you get what you think you deserve

to treat myself with the love, care & respect

that I wish to receive

from others

And to accept myself for who I am

So young
ready for life
but in order to begin
something must end
and now I will need
strength
& love
to rise
again

What is sleep?

Is it just to rest the body

while the mind runs free

don't remember any dreams

what are they anyway

are they significant

do they tell us about ourselves

or who we need to be

Where do our dreams go?

Do they vanish into thin air

or do they scream

do they cry

do they fight

why can't we hear them

when they try to escape

the prison that we made for them

Life has no secrets

the truths are only hidden

we just have to look

within ourselves

to find the answers

to the questions

few of us

dare

to ask

Schrödinger's cat
started out as a kitten
as most cats do
grew up to be a (mostly) normal cat
till one day
she found herself
in a strange predicament
living inside a box
with food to last a lifetime
everything she could ever want
but she was lonely
wanted a family
her only escape
could cause her death
what would you do
would you wait for someone else
to choose your reality
maybe we'll never know how it feels
to live in a state
of uncertainty
or maybe
we already do

It's not a good thing
to be the cat
stuck in a box
of uncertainty
you have to choose
which reality
is right for you
and commit to it fully
no room for doubts
or hesitation
maybe it's faith
but if you have to believe
in something
why not believe
that your dreams
can come true
don't leave it up to chance
make the decision
we create our past
& our future

they change slightly
with each
present

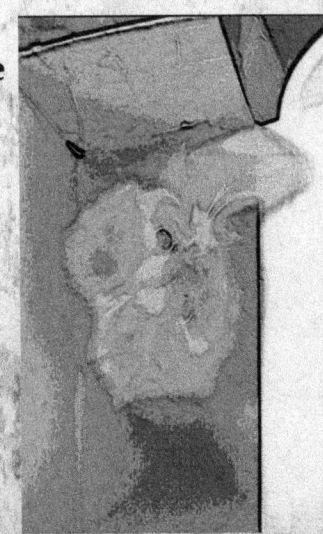

Sugar/Candy

We met at the club
after the audition
said she'd take me out
show me the ropes
I entered her world
the smell of sex
welcomed us
to a world where women
are just a commodity
and men feel it's okay
to touch & do what they please
because we only exist
for their pleasure
because we comply
and sell our selves
our souls
for nowhere near
what we deserve
And don't complain
when they treat us
like slaves

You thought you knew me
you took my heart
and lost it
only to find

emptiness

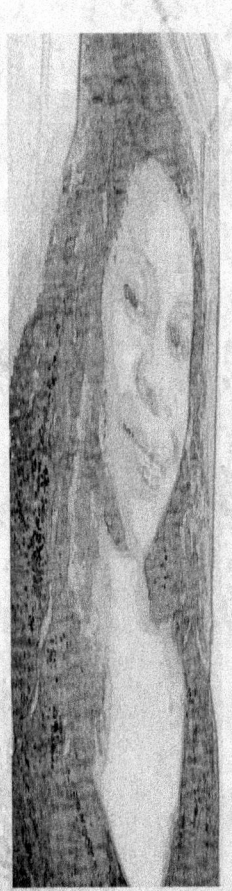

look at me
tell me what you see
am I what you always wanted

If you love someone
set them free
and if they come back
it was meant to be
if love is an ocean
then I am the sea
you are the one
who sets me free
I am the darkness
and you are the light
together we are both
part of the fight
I choose to love
out of necessity
I choose to hope, throughout the pain
because it is all I can do
to believe in you

Can I hold you forever in my mind

can we see the stars as they forget to shine

can we show them what's in our hearts

make them see that we're not blind

I wish I knew if you understand

if you still hold me close

hold me in your arms again

My vow is to
live life passionately
allowing myself
to feel
every emotion
effortlessly
it's what makes us human
our ability to feel
and understand
the what
& why
of it

What is Love?

To me it is:

when you care so much you would do

whatever it takes to keep them in your life

when you care enough

to do what's best for them

even if it may hurt you

when you would be there for them

no matter what

when you don't give up

when things don't go well

but also knowing

when to let go

it is the emptiness you feel

when they're not around

it is the excitement, the comfort, the peace

you feel

when they are

Your love is like a beautiful,

fragile, piece of dust that I wanna hold

in my hands but can never grasp

every time I see you feels like a dream

so elusive

ready to fade into that place

where lost dreams go

I need a reminder

that this is real

your kisses send chills through me

when we make love

time stops

and I treasure every moment

we spend together

so that they won't fade

and disappear

into that place

where lost dreams go

I remember moments

snapshots in time

that first time we met

the second

third, & fourth

I can remember

every single day

we spent together

so much that I could write a book

one day for each chapter

I write on paper
what I cannot speak
in words
I may not be able to
tell you how I feel
but if we share the same spirit
words cannot express
the passion in my soul

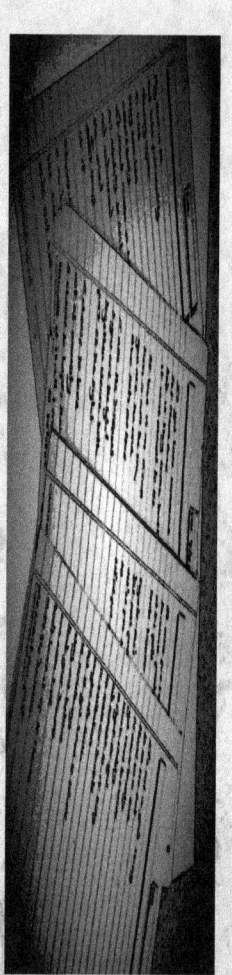

Fragmentation

Moments stolen

in a land where time doesn't exist

years of friendship

condensed

into days

I can count on 2 hands

can we build something real

out of stolen moments

attached by the strings

of our consciousness

can we transcend

the non-existence of time

and become

through these fragmented pieces

what we were always meant

to be

Close your eyes
& look at me
tell me what you see
I look at you
and see
my reflection

when we accept
a particular wave
as truth –
that reality comes into focus
It all depends
on what we believe
what we choose
to focus on
Believe in your own immortality
health & prosperity
The world is not chaos
nor is it random
pure randomness is theoretical
as in – only exists in theory
it is controlled & guided
by everything
that comprises it

The clouds comfort me
they look like soft cushions
my mind is clear
the fog has lifted
and I see
that I was living
in a fantasy
wishing you would be
the person of my dreams
but yet you are human
as well as I
and may not fit perfectly
into each others expectations
I see your shortcomings
I'm learning to accept them
& not judge you for them
because I know
I am not exempt
from scrutiny
and I would wish
to not be judged
for mine as well

Is it an irrational fear
that holds me hostage
in this metal prisoner in the sky
is it my fear
of losing control
or the visions
I see behind my eyelids
as I look out at the clouds
that appear to me
as real a possibility as any
If I create my reality,
am I creating my fear, my anxiety?
And can I not create it?
Trying to quiet my mind
how many possibilities are there
an infinite amount
until 1 is locked into focus
& becomes our reality
wave/particle duality
everything interacts as
a wave creating the interference patterns
of reality as we know it

Burn the flames licking at the wound

before it leaves forever

I see the traces of you in its eyes

the wound will never heal

I see the true reflection in your eyes

as the snake begins to move

time to turn ashes into dust

burn the snake before the coals

I know I've seen that smile before

time to hide behind the mask

darkness closing in on me

you stain everything you touch

I feel your arms encircle me

and I am trapped in your embrace

now that our masks are gone

I can see you clearly

and I see that smile again

It's the darkness that holds me to you

you can't tell me lies

you won't let me touch you

what are you afraid of

tell me the truth

I love you

I'm not going to take this pain

tell me now if you can hear

then you can forget me forever

because I just can't take the pain

I want to know

before I go insane

Maybe life is just one state of existence

I am the phoenix
a bird, transformed
rising from her ashes
once again free
from the darkness
from the world
from the bars from which
she once called life
free
to be herself
to break free from
her own imprisonment
and finally sleep
peacefully
but only
until
next
time

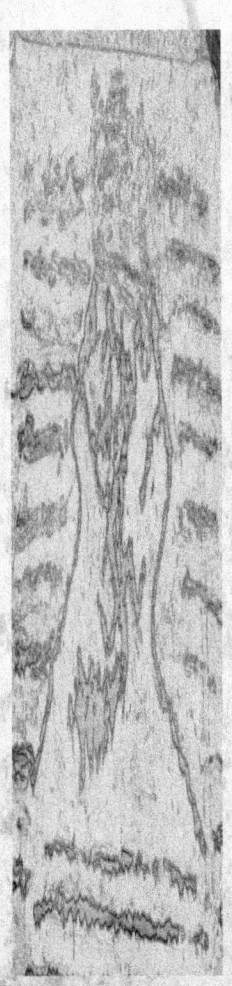

I write you

into existence

as soon as the words

appear

I see your

m o l e c u l e s

coalesce

and you

become

real

Tell me what I should do

should I follow before I fall

will I drown with in my tears

will they carry me away

with all the lost forgotten years

will they hold me in contempt

will they hold me when I fall

Tell me again

will you tell me

the truth

Apology

This is my apology
to everyone I know
I'm sorry if I let you down
I'm sorry if I'm not who you thought
I was
I'm sorry I'm not the person
you want me to be
I'm just me
you want my autobiography
do you want the official version
or do you want to get to know me
or maybe it's none of the above
maybe you just want to hear
my voice

they can't take my memories away from me

it seems like it was all a dream.

an impossible dream that never happened

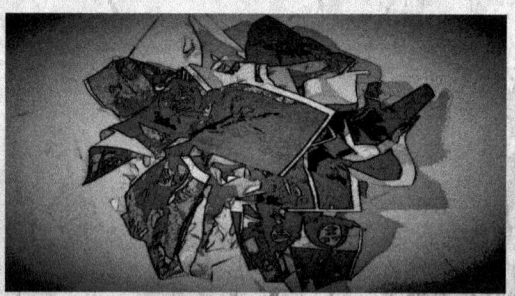

I don't know what brought us

into each others lives

but I think about you every day

you inspire me

to become whoever I want to be

There is no secret
to happiness
it comes
from just being
in the present
in the now
maybe we expect
it to overcome us
but I think
it's more of a feeling
of being at peace
with the world
our lives
& our selves

Sometimes I find it hard

to find logic

caught up in the ins & outs

of my mind

so hard to tell the difference

between what is real and what is

not

I want to hold you

I want to know you

feel you completely

I need you to be real

but are you only

in my mind

We are 2 strands

of a DNA molecule

attached

but not yet intertwined

Forever is a concept

I cannot fully grasp

it's too broad

too consuming

too permanent

death is always lurking

hiding

in the distance

we may never know

how close we come

every single day

I would paint the world

in bright colors

I would paint myself

happy

I would paint you

in the shadows

never directly seen

Feels like I'm in a dream...
more like a nightmare,
someone else's hell
tortured by emotions
unable to control

If you look into my eyes

can you see me

if you touch my skin

can you feel me

if you pierce my skin

can you hurt me

if you kiss my lips

can you taste me

and after all this

do you think you know me

if you look at me

will I disappear

The words

are not necessary

we know

how we feel

we know

we must follow it

that it will not

just go away

the words

are not necessary

we are in

each others parts

and in these parts

is the

hole

This is that feeling

that I never want to end

that always ends too soon

He is like Schrödinger's cat
to me
he simultaneously exists
and doesn't exist
because for me,
I can never know

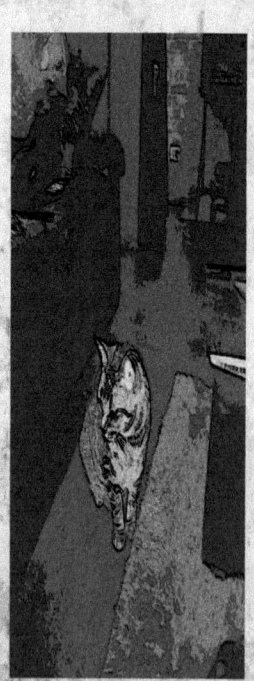

Like flying through jello
incomprehensible
inconceivable
the speed at which we are moving
It always scares me
I know it's because I believe
in all possibilities
no matter how great or small
the idea that air (which seems like nothing)
can hold us
but the molecules in air
comprise matter as well
and is not 'nothing' as it seems
it is actually no different
but then what of gravity?
$F=ma \ F/Fg$
air is not consistent, the particles vary
& are in motion
the air particles are us as well
I write to calm myself
to rationalize my fears
but it's the writing that calms me
not the rationalization
so I sit, writing; hoping the calm
doesn't lull me
into a false sense
of security

Trapped on a train
all alone
in a life
all my own

never there
open the wire
face the flame
too tired to force
back the face of shame

make me quiet
make me live
make it all
just never end

hope is broken
see the empty spoon
look at the lies
as they govern all that rules

make the darkness
become my home
make me face it
all alone

watch the light
and make me see
just what it is
that makes me free

hope is broken
understood
my heart is open
to empty wounds
makes them heal
empty spoons

everything is dark within
darkness falls
don't hide in sin
all the hours
that fade away
make nothing here
and nothing hides away

turn the tables
inside out
above it all
we all cry out
hope is broken
we all fear

seas the ocean
break away
now I see
what fades away

everything's broken
in my life
Hope is gone now
it will not return

make me see
when I am blind
that nothing heals
a broken mind

time is endless
in what it sees
we all are there now
it's time to be

nothing laughs
when darkness falls
all our hopes have
turned to dust

and we are buried
in the flames
our lives are endless
neverending

turning down
the ends of all
holding within itself
all that we
forget to keep

maybe they
will see the light
hold open the door
for the dirty flame

fear itself
is neverending
openness is full of lies
we are all here now

full of sadness
as the ends
begin to meet

we're all safe now
in the ending
hoping for what we find dear

making way
for empty landings
we pave the way
for all that's there

no one sees the aftermath
no one there could
see the glass

waiting on the steeple door
afraid to look/afraid to find
what they knew
was waiting there

hold your breath
suspend your fear
make everything
as unreal as it appears

then wait and see
and open the door
and look in the flames
at what is real

I don't see the light in the darkness
please come back to me
the world is on fire
I'm burning with the flame
she saw you coming you never...
I saw your face
you never looked back
at me
you never looked back
at the ashes you left behind
did you want us to know you
again?
Did you think we were blind?
The dog meets you again,
and you push it away,
like a disease.
I feel no pain anymore
fire took it all away
and now you're gone
I'll never know how you ended
there will be no more pain
till you...come...back
Did you know you died in my eyes years ago
I saw your face coming towards me
in the darkness
I saw the fire
I saw the flame
And you never came back
Did you?

Her eyes glazed over

as they told her the news

she knew it was over before it began

she had lost him again

and this time she knew

he would not come back

she could feel it when he came

to watch her

and her eyes were like stone

as she turned to face him

and as she screamed

she saw herself

in his eyes

The ice was frozen in her soul

breaking to pieces with every touch

through the thin covering, she lies

you see her through you

as she passes you by

she knew what happened

before I saw

and now your words call to me

haunt me

and like ice, I've turned cold

and bloody

and now

it's your turn

Close your eyes and watch

the darkness fade away

fire no longer dulls the pain

can you see the lizards dancing in disguise

do they see us? Can you see their surprise

we're on the outside looking in

how could we know

that their surprise

is really pain

You were the smile upon her face

it took a while for it to come

but now it's time to see the light

before the final words are spoken

before the final shade is drawn

tell me what is going on

tell me what is wrong

don't let the darkness take you away

before the final curtain is drawn

Your eyes told a story

of what we forgot

she held them up for all to see

it's hard to believe

who knew the end was near

it was so hard to see

the future is never clear

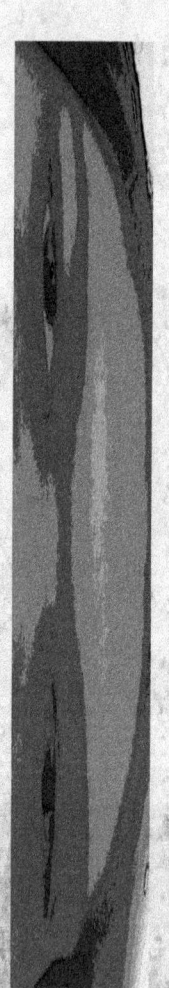

Can you see me in the darkness

can you see the pain I feel

do you leave me there alone

do you hold me till I drown

in a pool of tears I shed for you

or do you just walk away

unaware

that I lay drowning in the dark

or did you just not care

that I would sacrifice

my life for you

how could you be so calm

how could I still love you

after everything

we've been through

maybe I just wanted to believe

couldn't let go of the thought

that we were meant to be

You watch as I drown in a pool of tears
for you.
I hold you in my arms and think
of what used to be and why it is no more.
You are no different from them anymore
those who are lost in my memory
not wanting to disturb what has always been
it is too late for the time to be.
A long time has passed and I no longer exist
to you.
Where am I now, who do I belong to?
What is left of everything that matters
why are things the way they are?

Give me hope for what may come.
Hope is only a screen for the future,
for what may never come.
Put all your voices to the test.
Who do you think you are?
What happens when you find out
that you are not.
It is not ever as its seems.
Maybe there is nothing.
Cease to exist or to be,
who knows what is yet to come.

Blood fills the spaces that flow
through the skin, barely below the surface,
trying to get out at any opening.
We bleed for them,
for those in the darkness
who need it to survive.

No one tells us what is right or not.
Make me see the truth.

What can it be?
Why is everything doomed
to be the way it is in my mind
I see things how they are to me,
but there is no real way to be.

Who is this person underneath the skin,
the one who can see who has eyes of fire.
There is nothing that can be done.

Who is here to take my place.
Who will she be.
Why is there no reason for anything.
No one wants to believe that.
There is no beginning or end
or anything that we can see.

Darkness fills the spaces
underneath the bone,
hiding your lies under the fire,
sliding the dreams of unworthy rulers
into the time under the life.
Tell me the truth, what truth there is.
What is real.

Who is in the broken sky,
torn to pieces,
falling to the ground.
Why are they broken,

who were they once?

Nothing has meaning beyond what it is.
Tell me what lies beyond the fire,
beyond the light that fills the void
in all our lives.

Skulls in My Eyes

They told me everything they wanted to hear
my eyes search for shadows,
the skulls on the wall
my eyes have shattered
and the glass is all wrong
kill the pain with thunder, focus on the lies
I have to feel the pain
cause I don't know how to fall
a lizards tail running through my brain
tearing me apart
killing me again
I don't need friends,
the voices look for me inside my head
my eyes search for shadows,
the skulls on the wall
the eyes have shattered into the brain
icy thinness covers the fire in my soul
the candles burn within my eyes
your fear still hides beneath my skin
the wax falls from my skull like hair
painting your picture
my eyes are still inside of you

Fade Away

I try to watch without the fear

and hold on to what's left

the days are passing far away

and fire lights another chance for us

our days are numbered and fading fast

who knows where I am, and will it last.

Tell me am I dreaming,

my life is so unreal

holding me so tightly

the chances are fading fast

where are the ruins that show me the truth

the lies rise to the surface

and fire lights another chance for us

please tell me am I dreaming,

my life is so unreal

Poison Ivy

I am your soul,
though you walk over and through me
I make you see when I am blind
her lips are red and bloody
and though you love them
they are not real
you hold me deep inside of her
she tells me everything
though I already know
you cut through the thickness
and now I see that you are blind
just like me
who's gonna see for us now?

You've turned your back on reality
now her lips are reaching for you
her eyes are pulling you back
into her
I can feel you slipping away
now it's too late
and you know it too
you've lost the war
and I watch as her flaming hair engulfs you

This is just a photograph
of what no one else wanted
of the darkness
that calls itself home
only I can see what lies beneath
the hidden face looking out at me
you are the wooden smile on its face
you are its eyes between the sheets
black lies shining at me
telling me stories
of pain and suffering
that life was no addiction
the darkness smiled through that face
I saw the dream coming towards me
slowly descending
and the smile
screamed

Ever see the fire in your eyes
hold the flame with your tongue
watch the world disappear
into the darkness

can you feel me like I feel you
are you really inside of me
when you look into the future
can you see what I see

am I just imagining things
how can I tell the difference
between my dreams and reality
is my life just make-believe

how does what I've been through
compare to you
all I want is your respect
I want to know the truth

don't think I can't handle it
I'm stronger than you think
don't be afraid to hurt me
because pain is all I know

you taught me how to love
& that means more to me than
most
they will never understand it
but I will always knew

we were meant to be

close your eyes & look at me
tell me what you see
describe her to me
maybe then I can tell you if she is me

maybe then I will know how you see me
I wanna know the truth
maybe if I believe in my image of myself
maybe then you'll see me that way

did you ever believe in me
what happened to make you change
your mind
but I think I understand

why can't I let you go
this is not how
it's supposed to be
something's not right

sometimes I wonder
if you deserve
a second chance
and then I realize that's not what I want at all

I just don't want
to lose you

I wanna know what I meant to you
if you ever think of me
if you ever wish things were different

I'm trying to be honest with you
tell you how I feel
finally
but maybe it's too little too late

maybe you can still feel
the connection
if I send you a signal
will you hear it
are you still listening?

I guess all I can do is try
I know you can still feel it
still feel me
in your mind, your thoughts

how things could have been

I will always be there
maybe not how I am
but how you want me to be
maybe it's time to make
our dreams
a reality

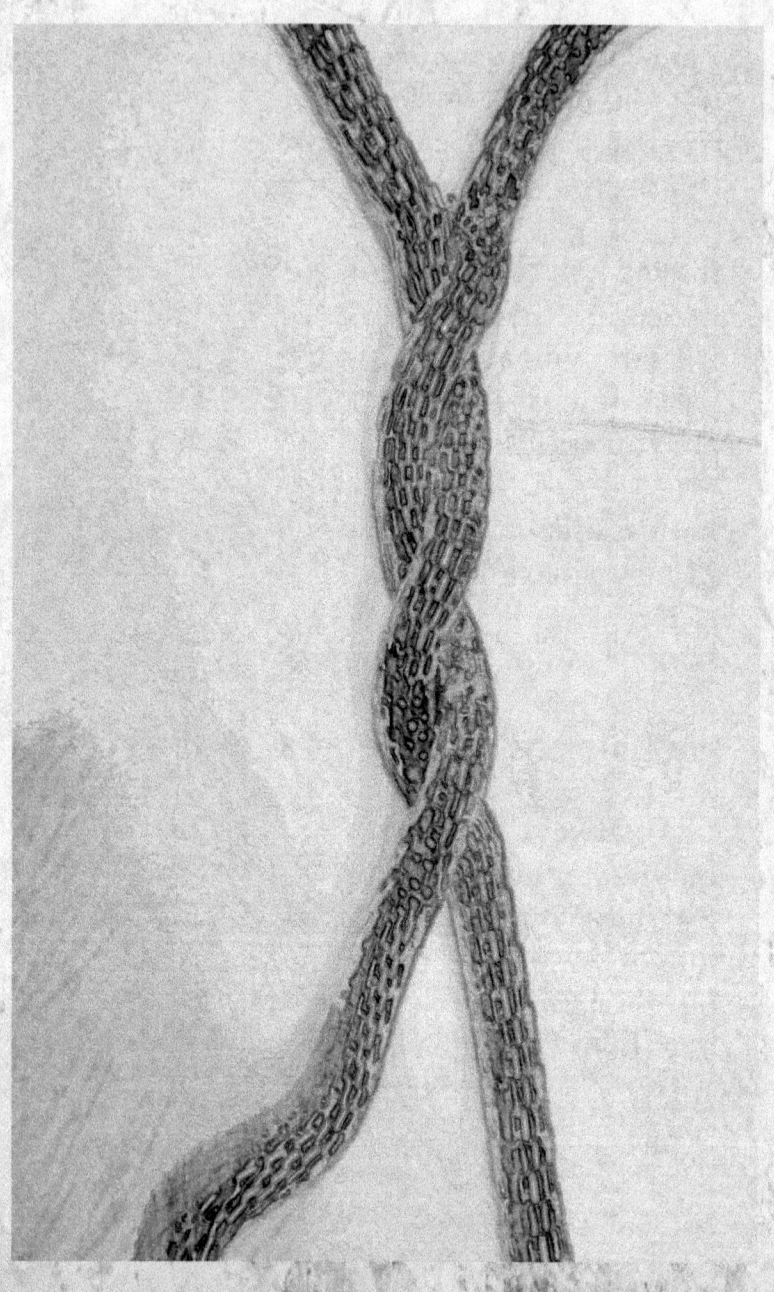

Sometimes I talk

to myself

you might think

I'm crazy

I'm not

I know there is

no one to answer me

so I pretend

that it's you

that it's someone

I can tell

someone

who will listen

to what I have

to say

You took me to a place

I remember it now

you opened my eyes

all I could see

was the brightness

You asked me the difference

only time will tell

what happened that night

why the stars chose

to shine so bright

or why

I walked

away

There is a song
that I sing
in my head
to you
It starts
with sadness
and as
you listen
to the words
inside my head
you hear it too
and know
that I only sing
the words
that have not begun
to fade

I know he is here
I can feel him surrounding me
my invisible friend
he's found me
led me
to the darkness
once again
pulling me in
deeper into his depths
my shadow friend
who never leaves my side
I still see you
hiding from the sun
you are my twin
always there
to lure me back
tell me that this
is where
I belong
but I somehow
always
see the light
and know
that you
will never win

I see the cracks

appear in your shadow

forcing the light through

you're becoming translucent

I can see straight through you

I can see that you are now blind

because you never wanted to see

never wanted to peel away

your outer layer

because now I see

your transparency

and there is

nothing

there

I look in the mirror
& wonder
who are you
are you like me
are you my twin
living in a parallel world
a parallel life
are you looking at me
through a shield
a shade
of distortion
can you pull me through
to your distorted version
of reality
I wonder
if I would know
the difference

I believe in a world
where the fantastical
is real
where every character
we know from movies
from books
really do exist
they have to
because they told us
their stories
they exist in a realm
we can only access
with our hearts
our souls
our spirit
no body is allowed
we see them
in our dreams
our fantasies
our imagination
and they are always there
timeless
always just as we imagined
waiting
for their stories
to unfold

You told me a story once
of heartbreak and truth
she told you her story
& you wrote it down
I think I read,
that book before
You told me
how she reached
right through the page
and broke your heart
pulled at the seams
sucked you in
to her black hole
you told me
that you could feel
yourself
falling
to
pieces
shredded
until you
were
just
words
on a
page
trying
to
escape

You tell me

that I am real

I am not an illusion

You did not create me

I chose to share myself

with you

You are just a medium

a vessel to illuminate me

I am not a character

in your story

you are the one

who is living

in a dream

world

a fantasy

a delusion

in your mind

You hold the pieces of my soul
opening them one by one
I can feel myself fading
as you try to put my pieces together
solve the puzzle
of me
But you forgot about the cracks
and there is no glue
strong enough
to hold
my pieces
together
And so they fade
as you watch
unable to fix
this effect
that you have caused
and I
am released
into the shadows
of your now broken
soul

I met a man once

in a dream

we sat

on building blocks

and talked

about any & every thing

I asked him all the questions

I ever wanted to know

and everything unknown

about the universe

He told me everything

and I understood

But when I returned

to my reality

I could not remember

a word he had said

just the memory

of a moment

of clarity

In my dreams
you're still alive
In my dreams
you came back

But you were different
not like yourself
it didn't matter
if you were
only a shade
of who I once knew
It doesn't matter
if you won't tell me
where you've been

I see images of bones
buried under the floor
fragments of blood
and secrets I do not know

I wish the fragments
were more clear
I see you
See all of you

what is it
that you are trying to tell me
that I can only remember
through the fragments
of my fading
dreams

A Dream of Banana Shoes

I had a dream once

that I went to the grocery store

and bought some

high heeled banana shoes

and then I lost you

I dream of you
bound to me
with invisible string
our thoughts
& hopes
& dreams
shared
across
vast amounts
of time
and space
It doesn't matter
how far
we are
as long as
I can trace
my invisible string
back
to
you

Maybe you were that little girl

that 5 year old ghost-bride

walking down

the spiral

staircase

dressed in

beautiful

shining

silver

disappearing

into the

fog

There is a place that I know
I used to live there once
in a dream
If I describe it to you
tell you how to get there
will you meet me?
The next time you find yourself
awake in a dream
take the spiral staircase
in the clouds
I will be near the top
dressed in silver
waiting for you
to take my hand
and lead me
to a place
that can only exist
if we believe
in it enough
to make it reality

You tell me

that reality is lost

that it left you long ago

and all that is left

are

traces;

pieces

of memories

shards

fragments

of

a

fading

dream

Index of First Lines

ABOUT THE AUTHOR

Latasha Day currently resides in California, but prefers to live in her dreams; and travel to faraway places, and do impossible things. www.ladylxa.com

www.ingramcontent.com/pod-product-compliance
Lightning Source LLC
Chambersburg PA
CBHW070750180626
46818CB00007B/3065